christmas promises

mia elliot

content warnings

playlist

Ariana Grande – True Love
Caleb Hyles – Love Like You
Taylor Swift – Paper Rings
Ruth B. – Dandelions
Andy Williams – It's the Most
Wonderful Time of the Year
Ariana Grande – Winter Things
Mariah Carey – All I Want Christmas
is You

Chapter 1
Lucy

THE PAST FOUR months felt more like a dream than a reality.

They had changed the course of my life forever—after getting back with Luke, I started a new job at Port-Cartier Elementary School. Going back to Seattle wasn't an option anymore, not with how my life finally came together, creating a perfect puzzle that I was content with. It all felt right. Shortly after deciding to stay, I made a quick trip to Seattle to pack up my belongings and sell anything I didn't want to bring. It was one last chance for Sailor and me to have a girls' road trip before we began living so far apart.

And while that was one of the hardest things I had to do, knowing that I had a home by Luke's side made it easier. It wasn't long before I moved in with him. We had spent ten long years apart, despite the love that always remained in our hearts.

"Why waste any more time?" Luke said, and I couldn't have agreed more. We knew we got along well, we knew we were meant to be, and we were ready to start living our lives together.

It all felt like the plot of a romance story—which I had

started reading again. In fact, my home library was full of them. My gaze wandered around the sage green room, with floor-to-ceiling bookshelves lining the walls. They were only halfway filled for now, but it was enough for me to settle in with a different good book every evening. In the corner of my library was the fluffiest white sofa ever known to man, where I spent many hours immersing myself in different stories that filled my heart with so much warmth. Now that I had found a way to believe in love again, these stories made me feel so good—to the point where Luke occasionally said I lived for my books.

That wasn't far from the truth—after all, I was living in my very own romance story.

As I heard the door downstairs open, I shut my book and hopped off my sofa. Luke was back from work, which was my favorite part of the day. Now that I worked at an elementary school, I had pre-specified holidays, but Luke wasn't as lucky. Lately, his work had been booming—which was both a blessing, since we needed the money for renovations around the house, and a curse because it meant we spent less time together.

Once I reached the ground floor, I found him in the kitchen, holding a paper bag from a Chinese place one town over. We had only gone there once, but the food was so good it left a lasting impression on me.

"No way!" I dashed toward him, leaning up to peck him on the lips. A knowing grin spread across his face as if he knew exactly how happy this would make me.

"Yes, way. Pick a movie, sweetheart, and I'll bring over the food."

He didn't need to tell me twice. In a heartbeat, I was in the living room, choosing a movie for us to watch. I picked a Christmas movie I had been dying to see to fit the winter theme.

When Luke brought in our noodles and the duck sauce, he

arched his brow at my choice. I, on the other hand, couldn't help but stare at him. How was it possible for him to be so handsome? I had spent months by his side, yet I still couldn't get used to the beautiful lines of his face and the warmth of his blue eyes.

"A Christmas movie?" he questioned as he placed the food on the small coffee table in front of us. Before I moved in, Luke didn't have a TV, claiming he didn't need one. But he did, exactly for evenings like this, so I could snuggle into his arms for a few moments before we dug into our food and focused on the movie entirely.

"Why are you surprised? It's past Thanksgiving so technically it's the Christmas season. Besides this is my favorite time of the year."

His expression scrunched in confusion, eyes curious as they stared at me.

"Is that so?" He ran his hand through my dark curls. I rested my leg on top of his, allowing myself to bask in the warmth his body radiated. I had always been a secret fan of Christmas time, even if I refused to admit it. For years, though, I forced myself to bury that passion deep inside me to avoid the painful memories linked with it. But now that we were back together, I could allow myself to enjoy this season to the fullest.

"Of course. Don't tell me you didn't know," I teased him with a playful nudge. "And here I was, thinking you knew everything about me…"

"You do manage to still surprise me every day, sweetheart," he said, handing me my noodles before they started cooling down. Curiosity still lingered in his expression. "I thought summertime was your favorite. At least, it used to be when we were dating ten years ago…"

"People change in ten years, Luke," I retorted, scooping up some noodles with my chopsticks. This hardly fit the winter theme, but they were so delicious I couldn't say no.

The exquisite taste melted on my tongue, awakening every single taste bud I had. "In more ways than one—I mean, it took you long enough to stop using three-in-one shower gel..."

Luke chuckled, his eyes crinkling at the corners. "Guilty as charged," he murmured, even if it was somewhat of a sensitive topic in our relationship. "No need to attack me, Luce. Instead, you can tell me why this time of year is your favorite..."

My mind instantly drifted back to when we first started dating. It was winter, and we were just kids, yet he somehow managed to make every moment feel so special that it stayed with me for the rest of my life. Luke seemed to have some kind of winter magic going on for himself. I could vividly recall us ice-skating, which I had always been terrible at, drinking hot cocoa, and staring at the Christmas lights together. It wasn't one big thing that made it special—it was a collection of moments combined to create an unforgettable experience.

"I thought you'd know. Come on, use those deduction skills in that big ol' head of yours..." I encouraged him, tapping the side of his head playfully. Luke thought for a moment, his brows furrowing in concentration.

"Was it because we started dating during winter?" he asked at last, and I shrugged my shoulders slightly.

"Partially. We had our first date around Christmas. I can still remember it so clearly...But then the next Christmas came around, and you did your best to make that one special as well. We went sledding with your parents and brothers and laughed until our stomachs hurt. And then, on Christmas morning, you gave me that scrapbook you made yourself..." My words trailed off as I recalled memories from ten years ago. Funnily enough, I had recently found some pictures from that period of our lives. "I don't know, those two winters were so amazing, and I just know that if we had stayed together, we could have…"

My voice broke a little at the reminder of everything we had lost. A small swallow disrupted my throat as I fought to keep my emotions at bay. I didn't want to get upset now. We were meant to have a chill dinner.

"Hey, hey…" Luke said soothingly, capturing my chin between his fingers and tilting my head up so I would look at him. The warmth of his tone struck me right at my heart, deepening the ache. How could I ever have thought that he didn't love me anymore? "No getting upset, sweetheart. We're back together now, and we have the rest of our lives to spend together. That's at least sixty more winters that I will make special for you. I promise."

A small, stifled laugh escaped my lips. This was one of his many talents—he could make me laugh anytime, anywhere. He leaned in, kissing my forehead and lingering there for a moment.

"That's a big commitment, you know," I teased, "because you've set up big expectations, and I'll expect you to top the previous year every time."

"And that is a challenge I gladly accept," he retorted with a cheeky grin before his lips dipped lower, kissing mine, only to pull away after two seconds. "I love you, sweetheart, but right now, you taste like beef pan-fried noodles, and I'll have to pull away."

All the sadness evaporated instantly as I grabbed him by the back of his head, pulling him in for another kiss. Our laughter blended with the collision of our lips on both ends, and at that moment, I knew this was right where I was meant to be all along.

Chapter 2
Luke

SNEAKING around Luce was proving to be quite the challenge. She was incredibly observant and fully immersed in the winter holiday spirit, so I had to plan each move carefully if I wanted to avoid getting caught. The truth was, I had known this moment was coming ever since I first laid eyes on her during her 'welcome home' party.

Somewhere deep in my heart, I knew we were meant to be —that we would find our way back to each other, just as I knew that I would marry her sometime soon. I didn't see any point in wasting more time when we both knew what we wanted out of life. We knew each other, inside and out, and I knew this was it for me. Nothing else could ever compare, and the only logical move was to move forward to the next step of our lives.

It began this afternoon, when Luce left for a school function, giving me a few hours alone to pull this off. I parked my truck in front of her mom's house and reached into my pocket to retrieve a small, velvet box containing a ring made just for her. It was a silver band with an oval-cut diamond, made with a lot of love and thought, and I knew she would adore it.

I should have felt some nerves, but instead, everything felt so natural that I could hardly wait for the moment to arrive.

I stepped out of the truck and walked up to the front door, knocking softly.

"Coming!" Eve's voice called from inside. After her injury this summer, she had taken quite some time to recover but was now doing much better, to the point where Luce had to remind her not to push herself too hard. Eve's face lit up with a smile as she opened the door, and her gaze landed on me. It was like seeing a glimpse of what Luce would look like in twenty-five years—soft facial lines, long, curly hair, and a warm, ever-present smile that I hoped to keep on Luce's face.

"Luke! I didn't expect to see you here," Eve said, her eyes scanning over my shoulder as she searched for her daughter.

"Luce isn't here," I explained. "She's at a school function, and I wanted to come see you on my own."

A hint of concern crossed her face as she stepped aside, gesturing for me to come in. In the living room, I found Ed lounging on the couch with a can of beer in hand, watching TV. He greeted me with a broad smile.

"Hey, Luke. Do you want to join me and watch the game?" Ed asked. Luce and I weren't the only ones making significant life changes—Ed had also moved in with her mom, and we couldn't be happier for them. Much like us, they were a perfect match, complementing each other in every way.

"Maybe some other time, Ed. I've got to talk to your lady," I teased, following Eve into the dining room, where we sat at the old, sturdy table. "I won't take up too much of your time, and I don't want you to worry that something's wrong." Eve's expression softened as I continued, "You know I love Luce more than anything in the world. Now that she's back in town—and back with me—I never want to let her go. Some might think we're moving too fast, but I've known that I wanted to marry her since high school. So, I'm here to ask for your blessing to propose to Luce. You mean the world to her, and therefore, your opinion means the world to me. I know I've messed up in the past, but—"

"Luke," Eve interrupted my pre-planned apology and assurances, reaching for my hand and giving it a reassuring squeeze. "No need to apologize. The past is in the past. If you two have let it go, no one will hold it against you."

I exhaled with relief, about to thank her, when she continued, "Besides, it's the twenty-first century. You don't need to ask for my permission. Luce knows what's best for her, and she's chosen you. So, if she's happy, I'm happy, and you have my full support to marry her." A wide smile spread across her face as she gave my hand a small tap.

This is going well, I thought to myself, smiling. *There wasn't even a hint of teasing...*

"But you know, it took you long enough," she added with a playful glint in her eye.

Ah, there it was. I couldn't help but laugh. "I agree whole-heartedly. But don't worry, I'm making up for it now."

After wrapping up my conversation with Eve, I had another important talk scheduled with someone else close to Luce. Once I got home, I video-called her best friend, Sailor. Sailor and I only briefly met when she helped Luce move her things to Port-Cartier. I had insisted on helping, but Luce said it was a 'girl thing' that I 'wouldn't understand.'

Sailor hadn't stayed long back then, but I looked forward to getting to know her better.

When she answered my video call, her expression was slightly confused, her gaze darting around as if she were trying to find Luce. We weren't on video-call terms yet, but I hoped that would change with today's conversation. After all, Sailor was a crucial part of my plan. I knew Luce would want her best friend to be there when she got engaged, and I was determined to make that happen.

"Hey, Luke," she said slowly, clearly unsure of the reason for my call. "Is Luce around?"

I shook my head, offering a reassuring smile. "Nope, just me. I know this might seem slightly out of the blue, but I'm reaching out because I need your help."

"Oh, my God!" she exclaimed immediately. I had to quickly lower the volume on my phone to recover from the sudden assault on my ears. "Is she pregnant? No—she'd definitely tell me first. I'd be the first to know!"

My brows arched in amusement. "I'd like to think I'd be the first to know, considering I'll be the baby's father, but no, I'm afraid I'm here to disappoint you. She's not pregnant— yet. But she is about to get engaged, and I really want to make sure you're there for that special moment."

I expected her to start screaming again, but instead, her eyes welled up with tears, and she sniffled loudly, taking a few moments to process the words I had just spoken. I watched her silently, giving her space to recover before speaking up.

"That is so sweet of you. And that would have been my next guess," Sailor assured me, her voice choked with emotion. Her recovery time was quick, because now, that infectious excitement was all over her face again. She clapped her hands together, nearly dropping her phone from whatever she had propped up against.

"I thought so," I said, smiling. "Anyway, I know this is kind of short notice, but I hope you can make it. I plan to propose to her on Christmas Eve, when our families will get together." They had always been our biggest supporters, cheering us on and hoping we'd end up together, so it only made sense that they should be there for this important step in our lives.

"Are you kidding me?" she waved me off with a grin. "I work from home, so I can make this work. Even if I didn't work from home, I'd still ditch work for my best friend's engagement. You can always find another job, but my best friend will only get engaged once…"

"Perfect," I said, feeling a great weight lift off my shoulders. One of my biggest worries was whether Sailor would be able to make it to Port-Cartier when I knew how much my girl would want her there.

"I'll send you an email with the available tickets I can book for you, so you can choose whichever one works best for you. I've also spoken to Eve, and she's more than happy to have you stay with her, so your accommodation is taken care of. I'd invite you to stay with us, but our guest room still isn't set up, and with everything going on, I can't—"

"Luke, relax," Sailor said, leaning back in her chair with a smile. "Staying with Eve is honestly the best thing you could have arranged for me. We love each other! She's like a mom to me. I'm going to have the best time." She waved off my concern. "But you don't need to get me a ticket. I can buy one myself…"

I shook my head firmly. That wasn't an option. It never had been. "Absolutely not," I insisted, pacing around the house. "I know I'm giving you short notice, and I'm the one asking you to come, so it's only fair that I cover the cost. I'll even have my older brother pick you up from the airport and drop you off at Eve's place. Everything will be sorted out; you just need to pack your bags and show up."

Sailor's grin widened. "Oh, wow. Luce wasn't kidding when she said you were a planner…"

I tilted my head, intrigued. "What else did she say about me?"

Sailor's smirk grew. "She's my best friend, Luke. I'm not about to spill all our secrets…"

"Fair enough," I laughed, glancing at the clock above the fireplace. "But she was right about one thing—I am a planner, and I have a lot to arrange right now. It's been nice talking to you, Sailor, and I'll see you soon. I'll shoot you an e-mail so we can sort out the plane tickets."

After we said our goodbyes and ended the call, I made sure to delete all traces of our conversation. I wasn't used to hiding anything from Luce, but I knew it would be worth it in the end. Now that I knew Christmas was her favorite time of year, I was determined to make the first one we spent together after ten years apart even more special than I had initially planned. I was committed to exceeding every expectation and making this moment one she would remember for the rest of her life.

Chapter 3
Lucy

IF SOMEONE ASKED me ten years ago where I saw myself working, I would never have guessed that I'd become a teacher at an elementary school. Initially, it wasn't my job of choice; it was more of a necessity born out of chance. After Luke and I broke up, my dreams fell apart; I was left adrift, so I chose something that seemed simple and accessible.

Now, I found it difficult to imagine myself doing anything else. I loved working with kids, especially here in Port-Cartier, where everyone knew everyone and was close with everyone. It created a sense of community like no other, especially with children. I didn't even mind doing the mundane things and sorting out the paperwork that came with my profession, mostly because I knew I would go home to a wonderful man who loved me.

Tonight, the said man had gone out of his way for our first Christmas in our new home. My mouth gaped open as I pulled up at our driveway, staring at the beautiful sight before me. At first, I couldn't believe it was our home and that he had done it all for us.

How did he even…

My thoughts faltered as I took in the breathtaking sight:

hundreds, if not thousands, of Christmas lights outlining our home. They were arranged with such precision and care that it must have taken hours to complete. As I stepped out of the car, still in awe, the lights twinkled as if on cue.

Through the window, I could see Luke grinning from ear to ear, holding a small remote controlling the lights. Tears welled up in my eyes, but I quickly wiped them away, not wanting him to see me crying. I'd been far too emotional lately, and I wasn't even sure why—perhaps because every little thing he did made me realize just how real this was. We were back together, and everything was falling into place.

The front door swung open, and Luke stepped out, rushing toward me. He greeted me with a kiss before pulling me into his arms, resting his chin gently on the top of my head. Together, we admired the breathtaking sight he had created.

"So, what do you think, sweetheart? Do you like it?" he asked, his voice filled with anticipation.

"I love it," I managed to say, struggling to keep my voice from breaking. "How did you even manage to do all this? It must have taken you hours…"

"A gentleman doesn't kiss and tell, Luce," he teased, his arms tightening around me. "I did have some lights planned, but after our conversation yesterday, I remembered how your face lit up when we walked through the streets and saw Christmas lights. I realized the amount I had gotten wasn't nearly enough, so I bought more. I wish I could take all the credit, but I did need Logan's help."

I sniffled for a moment, *thinking* I might be able to avoid full-on crying, but I was mistaken. Before I knew it, tears rolled down my cheeks, and there was no stopping them. Luke spun me around, his expression worried when he spotted the tears.

"Sweetheart?" he questioned, using his thumbs to wipe away the tears. "Did something happen? Did I do something wrong? Did—" Before he could flood me with further questions, I shook my head.

"No. No…it's nothing like that. It's just beautiful, and I'm so happy. I can't believe all of this is happening—that you're putting so much effort into making all of this so special…" I trailed off. Luke grimaced slightly, catching me off guard. I took a step back. Now, it was me who was worried. "What is it?" I asked. "Did something happen?"

"I just think you should prepare yourself for more crying, apparently. I didn't expect you to be this touched by all of this, so I have more things planned…"

"Luke!" I scolded him. "I thought we said we were keeping this Christmas simple!"

He flashed a cheeky grin. "We're keeping it simple, I promise. Come on."

As we stepped inside, I was enveloped by the comforting warmth of our home. It still felt strange to call it 'ours'—*our* home. It had transformed significantly from the days when Luke lived here alone. While he had decent taste, it was still very much a bachelor pad—functional but sparse, with little personality beyond the family photos and memories of our younger selves. Now, the space was filled with blankets and cushions, vases and plants, and, most importantly, enough cutlery and tea towels. *It felt like home.*

The fire crackled softly in the fireplace as I kicked off my shoes and slipped into my cozy slippers. Luke took my coat, as he always did when I came home, and guided me into the living room. On our coffee table, there was an Advent calendar with twelve bright red slots, each with festive Christmas patterns. The numbers were written in a familiar, chicken handwriting—Luke's.

I glanced back at him, my eyebrows raising in curiosity as I approached the coffee table. "What's this?" I asked, even though the answer seemed obvious.

"I wanted to give you something to look forward to every

day…aside from me, of course." He rested his hand on the small of my back, encouraging me to proceed. "Go ahead. Open the first one."

As I settled onto the couch, I carefully slid open the small slot on the Advent calendar, revealing something wrapped in festive Christmas paper. I was clueless about what it may be…until I started unwrapping it, and I got a better feel of the shape. It was a globe, and it wasn't long before I unwrapped it entirely, and everything set in my head.

Years ago, when we were kids, Luke's mom used to make the most beautiful Christmas ornaments. I remembered raving about them, completely amazed by how beautiful they were.

Linda had promised me one for the following Christmas, but life had other plans. Luke and I broke up before that promise could be fulfilled.

Now, I recognized the patterns I had admired all those years ago: a blue ornament adorned with tiny white deer scattered in all directions. In the center, written in Luke's familiar messy handwriting, was a message, *'Our First Christmas, Of Many.'*

I blinked rapidly, my gaze shifting between him and the ornament before I pulled him into my arms. I clung to him so desperately that he had to gently pat my back, his arms wrapping around me in a comforting embrace.

"If only I had known that an ornament would earn me this kind of hug, I would have done it a long time ago…" Luke said with a teasing smile, making me sniffle even more.

What was happening to me?

"Actually…" he continued, his voice taking on a more mischievous tone, "now that I think about it, I hope it will earn me something else, too…" Before I could fully process his words, Luke picked me up and tossed me over his shoulder. My sniffles turned into a small squeal as I carefully set the ornament down on a nearby table. Laughing, I wiggled slightly as he carried me into our bedroom. This day couldn't get any more perfect.

When my eyes fluttered open the next morning, I found Luke already awake and sitting by the side of the bed. He held the familiar little red box that marked day two of my Advent calendar. I rubbed my eyes, sitting up slowly, but for a moment, the Advent calendar was the last thing on my mind. All I could think about was how incredibly lucky I was to have Luke by my side.

In the past, I had never been one to connect or commit easily, or so I'd believed over the past decade. But now, reconnecting with a man who knew how to love me so deeply had changed everything. It seemed all it took was finding the right person to unlock a love that felt both familiar and new.

"Seems like you're even more impatient than I am," I said softly, reaching for the box. He responded with a smile, settling down beside me as he watched me open the slot.

To my surprise, the box felt unusually light, almost as if it were empty. But as I peeled back the wrapping and opened it, I discovered there was indeed something inside.

My gaze landed on two tickets for a sleigh ride. I gasped. This, too, was one of the reasons why I loved wintertime so much. It was one of the two occasions when they organized sleigh rides down Main Street, which I thought was magical. The sleigh rides were also one of our earliest dates and one of the more memorable ones.

"I can't believe this…" I trailed off, shaking my head in disbelief. "Seriously, how did you come up with all of this?"

"Sweetheart, things like these come naturally when you're with the woman you love," Luke said, his tone soft. "I've got plenty more where that came from, so try not to get too emotional today." He nudged me playfully, and I took that as my cue to leap onto the bed, straddling him with a grin.

"I don't think I like your tone, Luke…" I teased, my eyes sparkling with mischief.

A boyish grin spread across his face as he smirked at me. "Oh, yeah? What are you going to do about it?"

"I have an idea or two…"

As six p.m. rolled around, we headed down the long road leading to the inn that hosted the sleigh rides. This event only happens once a year during the holiday season. Dozens of cars were parked in the parking lot as people milled about on the covered porch. Everyone was bundled up, as Port-Cartier was chilly at this time of year.

And Luke came prepared.

"You just need to sit back and let me handle everything," he said when I offered to help. True to his word, he had come well-equipped: blankets, cushions, and a small basket of snacks for us to enjoy. Although technically, it wasn't allowed to bring outside food, he insisted the quality of the hot chocolate there had seriously declined.

I glanced at the basket in the back seat, a smile tugging at my lips, before meeting Luke's gaze again.

"I'm seeing more and more of your bad boy side," I joked, "and I have to admit…I'm quite intrigued. I didn't know you had it in you."

As Luke parked in a spot, he rolled his eyes playfully but quickly leaned in to steal a kiss. I met his lips with a smile, brushing mine gently against his before leaning in for another, deeper kiss.

His grin widened as he pulled back slightly. "Luce, please. Control yourself. I'm just trying to reach the basket and the blanket," he teased me.

Despite the piercing chill outside, I felt nothing but warmth—nothing but love. I didn't even know it was possible to be this happy, but with Luke, I learned something new every day.

Chapter 4
Luke

EVERYTHING WAS GOING ACCORDING to plan. The Advent calendar I'd made kept Luce both distracted and excited, allowing me to work on the bigger surprise I had in the works. The tickets for Sailor had been arranged, Landon had agreed to pick her up when she landed, and Eve had already prepared the guest bedroom for her arrival.

I had also been spending extra time in my workshop, determined to have the home library completed before Christmas. When Luce moved in, she hadn't specified many requirements for our new home—aside from the décor, which, to be fair, did look great. But the library was non-negotiable. She had even brought along eighty books from Seattle, after not wanting to part ways with them. She assured me that she had to leave most of her collection behind, but these were the books she didn't want to separate from. And if it was important to her, it was important to me, too.

After my shower, I headed downstairs and found Luce sitting at the kitchen table with a cup of tea cradled in her hands. I raised an eyebrow in surprise.

"No coffee, sweetheart?" I asked.

She shook her head, bringing the mug to her lips and

savoring the warmth of the liquid. Luce was always beautiful to me, but in these tranquil moments—her hair pulled up in a messy bun, wearing nothing but my t-shirt—she took my breath away. I still couldn't believe she was by my side again.

"My stomach's a bit off this morning," she explained. "So I thought it would be better to skip the coffee and go for tea."

"I'm sorry to hear that." I stepped closer and placed a gentle kiss on her temple. "You still haven't opened the third slot?"

"Of course not," she replied with a smile. "I was waiting for you…"

I set my mug into the coffee machine. Despite Luce opting for tea this morning, coffee was my lifeline. With so many things on my agenda, it was the only thing keeping me functioning these days.

"Go ahead," I said, noticing her excitement. "I can see how impatient you are."

She placed her mug down and practically leaped across the room to her Advent calendar. Her eyes were bright as she picked out the box marked with a three—which, granted, looked suspiciously a lot like a nine. Her face lit up the moment she realized what it was.

"A reservation at *Sunny Bird*?" Luce exclaimed, her eyes widening as she looked at the small card inside the box. "Luke, the waitlist for that place is six months…how did you manage to pull this off?"

I chuckled at her shock. For a small town like Port-Cartier, that waitlist did seem outrageous. But *Sunny Bird* had earned its reputation as a must-visit spot, drawing in not just locals but tourists from neighboring towns as well. Supposedly, the food was *that* good.

"I'm sorry, but that information is strictly confidential…" I smirk as the coffee machine behind me huffed and puffed, signaling that my coffee was ready. I took a sip, letting the rich, warm liquid awaken my senses before I continued, "I know winter is your favorite time of the year because of all the memories we've shared over the past ten years, so I thought it would be nice to create some new ones, at new places, ten years later, so…" I approached her, kissing her forehead. "I'll come by to pick you up from work around six. Make sure you're ready, sweetheart."

At precisely six p.m., I pulled up in front of our home. I had showered at work and brought a change of clothes from home earlier that day. I knew it was silly, but with all the time we spent away from each other, I wanted her to feel that yearning and anticipation of me picking her up for a date all over again. Living together was amazing—everything I ever imagined it would be like, and more—but I wanted to make sure she didn't miss out on anything.

When Luce stepped out onto the front porch, she looked stunning. She wore a gray coat over a cream blouse with a floral pattern and sleek black trousers. Her outfit wasn't revealing, but it was enough to make my mind short-circuit with desire. The red lipstick on her lips only heightened the effect, making my thoughts swirl.

I stepped forward, extending my hand toward her with a smile. "Your boyfriend is one lucky man, you know," I clasped my fingers around hers. She tried to hold back her smile, but the way her lips twitched gave her away.

"My boyfriend is also a silly goose," she teased.

I raised an eyebrow. "If I remember correctly, you're the one with the goose nickname…" I said, recalling how Logan had come up with it. I couldn't remember the reason behind it, but it had stuck around until now.

We made our way to my truck, and the ride was thankfully short. Fifteen minutes later, we arrived at the restaurant and were seated at our table. A soft candle flickered between us, casting a warm glow on Luce's face and making her look almost ethereal.

"Stop staring at me," she scolded me.

"I'm sorry," I said, though I wasn't sorry at all. "You just look so stunning tonight. I can't take my eyes off you…"

Just then, the waitress arrived, coming to her rescue. "Welcome to Sunny Bird," she chirped brightly. "What can I get for you tonight?"

We both turned our attention to the menu. I had chosen this place because of its wide assortment of house-made pasta, something I knew Luce would love. Since she moved in, we'd upped our carbonara consumption at home, but I figured we should enjoy it somewhere special as well. It was an easy choice, and I was glad to see her excitement about it.

"I'll have sparkling water and your carbonara pasta, please," I said, handing the menu to the waitress. Luce's eyes lit up at the mention of her favorite dish.

"I'll have the same," she agreed with a smile.

As soon as the waitress walked away, Luce's smile widened mischievously. "A man after my heart…"

I reached for her hand, gently stroked it. "Always." I smirked. "Their pasta is supposed to be incredible, so I thought it would be perfect for tonight."

Luce arched an eyebrow playfully. "Are you just trying to buy my love with pasta, Luke?"

"I don't need pasta to buy your love, sweetheart"—I grin —"but it certainly doesn't hurt…"

Being with her felt so effortless, so natural. It was everything I had longed for my entire life. After experiencing it during our teenage years, I spent all the time we were apart searching for that same connection. But I couldn't find it anywhere else—only when I was with her.

"Mm, you're right," she said, her eyes sparkling. You have

many charming qualities, like how handy you are with wood..."

I knew exactly where this was going. Every other day, Luce would come to me with an inspiration photo and expect me to bring her ideas to life in our home. I loved every minute of it.

"Miss Milburne," I said with a playful tone, "I can't keep working for you for free. If you want to hire me for my services, you will have to offer some kind of payment."

She rolled her eyes, giving my hand a light, playful slap as the waitress arrived with our sparkling water. Usually, Luce would pair her meal with a glass of wine, but I noticed she'd opted for the sparkling water tonight—probably because her stomach was still a bit tender.

"Isn't my presence payment enough? I mean, think about it. You're doing this for your future wife..."

I did my best to hold back a smile. We'd talked about marriage and kids, and we were both clear about what we wanted from life. It was simple: a beautiful home, two kids, and a dog down the road once we were married. Little did she know that part of that plan would be unfolding sooner than expected.

"Future wife, huh?" I teased, leaning in slightly. "Does this mean you're already planning on marrying me?"

Before she could respond, the waitress arrived with our plates. They were the largest portions of pasta I had ever seen, but I had no doubt Luce would devour hers—that was the extent of her love for pasta. It looked absolutely delicious, too.

"Of course," Luce replied, diving into her pasta. "There's no one else I'd rather spend the rest of my life with. I think we both knew from the moment we were young; it just took us a while to figure it all out."

It did, but I liked to think everything was happening for a reason—including this. Now that we were together, we were stronger than ever, with our lives all figured out.

"I'll take that into consideration," I said with a hint of teasing in my voice, "and I will also do whatever you need me to around the house. I'm happy to make all your dreams come true, sweetheart."

The smile that appeared on her face lit up the entire room, making every word I just said a promise to myself. "That's good, really good…"

From the tone of her words, I could tell she had more plans up her sleeve, and I was eager to help bring every one of her projects to life. After all, I just wanted to spend the rest of my life making her happy.

After our fulfilling dinner, we were both barely able to move. The pasta had been delicious but also quite heavy, leaving us barely able to move. My hand rested comfortably on her thigh as we drove home, my focus on the road ahead.

To stretch out our evening a bit longer, I decided to take a different route home—through the forest and past the small grassy clearing that would soon be covered in snow. Normally, this spot was empty, but tonight, it was filled with cars and a collection of Christmas trees, ready to be taken home.

A Christmas tree—something Luce and I had talked about but hadn't yet gotten around to picking out.

Instantly, she patted my shoulder with excitement. "Oh, my God, Luke. Christmas trees! We should stop and get one. We need to do it anyway, so we might as well do it now…"

My stomach protested at the thought of moving more than necessary, but her enthusiasm was contagious and impossible to resist. I pulled over to the side of the road and, after we both got out of the truck, approached the elderly gentleman who was managing the Christmas tree lot. He greeted us with a friendly nod as we walked up, and I could see Luce's eyes washing over the trees with eager anticipation.

"Looking for a nice Christmas tree, folks?" the elderly gentleman asked with a warm smile. Luce nodded eagerly, her excitement evident. She wasn't joking when she said Christmas time was her favorite—I hadn't seen her this excited in a long time.

"Yes," she said. I've wrapped my arm around hers, placing a small kiss on top of her head.

"It will be our first Christmas together," I explained to the old man, "so we're hoping to find a special tree."

The man's eyes twinkled as he ran a gloved hand through his thick white beard. "Well, you've come to the right place, especially if it's your first Christmas together. And congratulations," he said cheerfully, "We've got to make sure it's a nice one. Feel free to look around, but I have just the tree for you, too…" He made a sweeping gesture for us to follow him, and we did.

In the back, hidden behind dozens of other trees, stood the perfect one: wide branches and the most stunning shade of green I had ever seen. I glanced at Luce, and her face lit up with pure joy. It was clear we were taking this tree home. We didn't need to exchange any words. As our eyes met, she gave a slight, definitive nod, silently confirming that this was the one.

We didn't need to look at any other trees.

"We'll take it, boss," I said.

"Tony! Mac!" the old man called out two guys who looked like they were his sons. "Help us load this tree onto the gentleman's truck."

"Right away, pop!" one of them responded as they moved toward us.

I reached for my wallet to pay, but the old man quickly shook his head. "No, absolutely not. This tree is going to your home without any payment. It's the first Christmas you two are spending together, and this is my gift to you…"

"No way." Luce grabbed my wallet out of my hand. "That's incredibly kind of you, but you have a business to run, and I can't let you lose money by the end of your shift— especially not during Christmas time."

God, I love this woman.

The old man looked at me, a soft glint in his eyes. "She's got a lot of spirit, doesn't she?"

I chuckled. "You have no idea. I'd listen to her if I were you. She's the boss around here, and she always gets her way."

"All right, all right," the old man said, raising his hands in a gesture of surrender. "No free trees for you this year…"

The tree was eighty dollars, but Luce somehow managed to press a hundred-dollar bill into the old man's hand, insisting he keep the change for his kindness. Tony and Mac loaded the tree onto the truck, and with a final wave, we headed home, surrounded by Christmas lights and so irrevocably in love.

Chapter 5
Lucy

WHILE I THOUGHT food from *Sunny Bird* was incredible last night, the next morning, my entire body protested at the thought of ever eating pasta again. I spent the majority of my morning in the bathroom, slumped by the toilet, and it took me quite some time to gather the strength to stand back up.

Luke knocked on the door a few times, offering his help, but I assured him the best thing he could do was give me some space. He reluctantly agreed and settled in the living room, waiting for me to come out.

By the time I got there, he had already set some of the essentials in the room—a cup of chamomile tea, a heat pack for my stomach, a warm, fuzzy blanket draped over the couch, and a Christmas movie playing softly on the TV.

I let out a small groan as I shuffled to the couch, where he greeted me with open arms.

"You don't look too good, sweetheart," he said gently, tucking a stray curl behind my ear. I melted into his embrace, too weak to move anywhere else. "Should I call Landon to come check on you?"

"No, it will get better. I'll be fine," I reassured him. While Landon was a doctor and dealt with far worse things daily, the last thing I wanted was for him to see me in this state. "If it doesn't pass in a day or two, then I'll reach out to Landon for help. Deal?"

He nodded, guiding me gently to the couch. There was one thing that made the day more bearable—my Advent calendar. As I sank into the blanket's warmth, I made a mental note to steal his idea for next year. Everyone should experience a love like this at least once in their lifetime, and I was determined to make it happen for him, too.

Today's slot in the Advent calendar was lighter than expected. I was anticipating another reservation, something we could perhaps hold off on until I was fully recovered. Instead, I found a tiny note in Luke's chicken handwriting. It read, *'go to the librati.'*

I squinted at the note, trying to make sense of what a *'librati'* could be. It was a term Luke had never mentioned before—was it a new store or a restaurant? My mind raced, but I couldn't come up with anything.

"Luke...why don't you take me to this *librati*?" I asked.

Luke took the card from my hand, inspecting the words with a bemused expression. "Luce, it says 'library,'" he said flatly. "Go to the *library*."

"Oh..." I pressed my lips into a thin line, offering him an apologetic smile. In my defense, his handwriting was so narrow it was hard to read. Landon might be the family's doctor, but Luke had a doctor's handwriting. "Sorry. That was my bad."

I flashed him a smile before standing up and heading into the library. My sickness was pushed to the back of my mind for a few moments of excitement. The moment I opened the door, my gaze was immediately drawn to the new rolling library ladder.

My mouth gaped open in sheer belief. I had mentioned a few times that I wanted one, given the size of our shelves, and Luke promised that he would make me one...but I didn't expect it to happen so quickly—not with all the work he had been doing around the house. This certainly wasn't on the list of priorities, or at least, I hadn't thought it was.

For a moment, my stomach issues were forgotten. I turned toward him and pulled him into a tight hug, my heart pounding with so much love it felt like it might burst.

"I can't believe you did this. Oh, my God. When did you even find the time…" I trailed off, overwhelmed, as he placed a gentle kiss on my temple.

"It's been a secret project I've been working on for a while. You spend a lot of time here, so I wanted it to be perfect for you. Go on," he said with a playful tap on my ass. "Try it out before I take you back to the living room."

He didn't need to tell me twice. A few long strides brought me to the rolling ladder, and I climbed onto it, letting it glide smoothly across the sleek floor. The motion felt absolutely glorious—I could hardly believe I finally had my own rolling ladder.

"Thank you. Seriously. I don't even know…" I shook my head as I hopped off the ladder. "I don't even know what I did to deserve all this…"

"You didn't have to do anything, sweetheart. Your existence has always been enough," he said. I wanted to kiss him, but the sudden wave of nausea reminded me why that might not be the best idea, so I held back. Instead, I took his hand and headed back into the living room, eager to spend a little more time snuggled up with him before he had to leave for work.

I had hoped the sickness would have eased by the next morning, but it hadn't. It looked like yesterday would repeat itself—I'd spend most of my day glued to either the couch or the toilet. Luke wanted to stay with me to take care of me, but I insisted he go to work. It was best for him to focus on his job while I concentrated on getting better in peace without him witnessing me at my grossest.

By the time he got home, I had managed to shower and wash my hair, though I didn't have the energy to go through my full curly hair routine.

"Hey, sweetheart." His voice echoed through the house as he unlocked the front door. "Are you feeling any better?"

Luke required regular updates throughout the day, and it had been an hour since my last one. My condition hadn't changed drastically—I was still sprawled out on the couch, wrapped in a blanket, with a cup of lukewarm tea on the coffee table.

"I'm okay. I feel...slightly better," I said as he walked into the living room. How he managed to look so good while I felt so awful was beyond me. He wore black jeans, a white shirt, and a leather jacket, with his brown hair slicked back. Everything about him made me want to rip his clothes off and jump on him right there and then.

"I'm glad to hear it. You look a little better, too." He set down a tote bag he had been carrying. A scent spread through the room—one that instantly piqued my interest in the best way possible.

"What do you have over there?"

"I brought you some soup," Luke replied. "Eve insisted I stop by on my way home and bring you some of the pumpkin soup she made."

They weren't joking when they said mothers knew best. Pumpkin soup sounded like the perfect remedy, especially when Luke heated it up and brought it to me, along with a water bottle to keep me hydrated. By the time I finished the comforting meal and took in some much-needed hydration, I felt significantly better.

Luke gestured toward the Advent calendar. "You haven't opened today's slot," he pointed out. "Did you want to do it now?"

"I do, but if it's another date somewhere, I will have to request a rain check. I hope you won't mind…"

"You're in luck, then, because it is not another date. In fact, it's something I think you may find useful…" Without any further prompting on his end, I reached for the fourth slot and opened it up. Again, it was a note from Luke, though this time I could read the letters much more easily—*'a spa date at home.'*

I smiled up at him. "As long as you don't mind that I have been sick the whole day…"

"You think a little bit of vomit will stop me from having a good time?" He shook his head. "You better think again." He stood up, his expression determined. "I will, however, need a few minutes to sort everything out before I come back to take you for your date. Will you be okay being on your own for a few more minutes?"

With a light shove against his shoulder, I pushed him away playfully, signaling that it was fine. "I spent the whole day on my own. Go, I'll survive a few more minutes," I reassured him.

Luke practically vanished after that—whatever he had planned took up all his attention and determination. When he reappeared about ten minutes later, he was shirtless, only in his pants. Despite my sickness, I couldn't help but be distracted by his effortlessly attractive appearance.

"Come on. Let's get you to the bathroom," Luke said gently, approaching me and scooping me up from the couch.

"Real romantic," I murmured into his shoulder, wrapping my arms around his neck to hold him close. He smiled but refrained from saying anything as we headed into the guest bathroom—the only bathroom in our home with a bathtub.

As we stepped inside, I was met with a sight that took me

completely by surprise. The bathtub was filled with soapy water, and the air was infused with a soft lavender scent. The room was dimly lit, with candles flickering softly around the tub. I hadn't expected this level of care and thoughtfulness, especially given how I'd been feeling.

"Luke…" I started. He always managed to know what I needed when I needed it.

He didn't respond, focusing solely on me as he carefully set me down. He began undressing me with deliberate tenderness, starting with the oversized sweatshirt I had borrowed from him, then the sweatpants. As he removed each layer of clothing, the brush of his fingers against my skin made me shiver, igniting a deep, aching need for him.

Once he had undressed me, he helped me step into the bath. I had wanted to take a bath earlier but didn't have the energy, so this felt like the perfect gift. The warm water enveloped me, soothing my muscles and relaxing every fiber of my being as I leaned back and closed my eyes.

"A date requires two people to participate, you know. You should join me…"

"That was originally the plan," he explained as he picked up a washcloth and gently dragged it across my skin. That soothed me even more. "But I am participating in my way. I want to take care of you, to make you feel good, and judging by the expression on your face right now, I'm doing a good job…"

A small exhale left my lips. Luke paid attention to every inch of my body, caressing it with the washcloth until he was all done cleaning me up, and helped me step out of the bath again. I didn't know what he had put in the bath, but I could swear I felt even better. Maybe it was the combination with the pumpkin soup—I couldn't tell.

He helped dry me off with a towel and then guided me into our bedroom. A smile tugged at my lips.

"I know I said I'm feeling better, but I'm not feeling *this* better," I teased, still wrapped in nothing but a towel, as I gestured toward the bed.

Luke laughed, retrieving a moisturizing cream I hadn't seen before.

"Don't worry, that's not what I have in mind. At least… not yet," he joked. I gestured toward the cream he was holding.

"Where did you get that from?" I asked, intrigued. The vanilla scent was inviting, and it looked like it was from a high-end brand.

"I picked it up specifically for moments like this. I went out to get it before I came home. Now, lie down so I can keep taking care of you."

I did so without any more protest. When I lay on the soft, freshly washed sheets of our bed—courtesy of Luke this morning—he gently flipped me onto my stomach and positioned himself carefully on top of me, making sure not to put any of his weight on me.

His strong hands glided over my body, applying just the right amount of pressure to ease every knot that had formed from stress. The sensation was incredible, making my mind relax and melt under his touch. I had no idea where he had learned to give such a perfect massage, but I was grateful for it. He seemed to hit every right spot, touching me just the way I needed. I didn't want him to stop. Small moments like this were certainly something I saw myself getting used to by his side.

Chapter 6
Luke

THE SIXTH OF my Advent calendar came around, and Luce felt much better. This morning, she had even made herself some breakfast, and strolled around the backyard. Despite her improved condition, she still wasn't entirely back to her old self, so I insisted she take it easy. Seeing her no longer dealing with nausea was a relief, which gave me peace of mind as I set out to run some errands—though 'errands' didn't quite capture the significance of my tasks for the day.

First on my list was a visit to my parents and brothers. With the proposal date fast approaching, I wanted them to be aware of my plans. They would be there to share in the moment, but I felt they deserved a heads-up with how much they had been cheering us on.

I parked the truck in front of my family home and didn't even have to ring the bell before my mom appeared on the front porch, waving enthusiastically. As I got out of the truck and walked toward her, she glanced behind me, expecting to see Luce with me. It seemed to be a common assumption lately—people assumed Luce went wherever I did.

While I would have loved for Luce to be here, I was glad

she chose to rest at home today. It gave me the chance to do this without any rush.

"Oh, come here. Give me a hug," my mom said, wrapping her arms around me even though we saw each other almost every day. "Where's Luce?"

"She's at home, still not feeling her best," I said, pulling my mom into a hug. I held her tightly before releasing her. Just then, Logan appeared at the bottom of the stairs, his arms crossed over his chest and a cheeky grin on his face.

"Well, well, well...look who the cat dragged in. Mr. Lover Boy," he teased. "Welcome home, Luke-Puke." I exhaled softly, knowing asking him to stop calling me that was point-less. Showing any annoyance would only fuel him to tease me more. Instead, I followed my mom inside.

"Is Landon here, too?" I asked, remembering he'd mentioned taking a few days off to spend with the family. Landon stepped into the hall as if on cue, hands stuffed in his pockets and an all-knowing older brother look on his face.

"I'm here, too, bud." My dad's voice rang out from the living room. With the entire family gathered, I finally had the chance to share my news with them.

"Why don't we move to the living room?" I asked, gesturing toward the room at the back of the house. I wanted everyone seated down for what I was about to say—and by everyone, I mainly meant my mom. Her eyes immediately filled with concern, but I was quick to soothe it. "Nothing bad has happened. On the contrary..."

We all made our way to the living room. My mom sat beside my dad, while Landon leaned casually against the wall. Logan plopped down on the sofa across from my parents and was about to prop his feet up on the coffee table, but a sharp look from my mom made him reconsider. He promptly obliged her rules, keeping his feet firmly on the floor.

"All right, everyone. As you know, Luce and I are hosting

Christmas Eve dinner this year, and you're all invited—Ed and Eve, as well as Luce's best friend, Sailor. We're looking forward to having everyone together, but there's another reason I wanted to bring this up now." I paused momentarily. "I'm planning to ask Luce to marry me. I've already spoken to her mom and chosen a ring—"

"Oh, God!" my mom cried out, her excitement loud enough to temporarily deafen everyone in the room. Her face was beaming with happiness, and she almost threw herself into my arms, hugging me tightly. "Luke, that's such wonderful news! I always knew you two would get married someday. I'm so thrilled it's finally happening. You and Luce are just perfect for each other! We'll have a wedding in the family—and who knows, maybe even grandchildren soon! I can't believe this—"

"All right, Linda, take it easy," my dad said, standing up from the couch. Though he was clearly excited, his demeanor was far more restrained compared to my mom's. He approached me with a smile and gave me a firm pat on the back once I managed to free myself from my mom's embrace. "I'm happy for you, son. Luce is wonderful. You two will have a wonderful life together." None of this came as a surprise, but it was still nice to hear how much they all loved her—how much they supported my decision to marry her.

I then turned to my brothers. Logan was the first to approach, grinning from ear to ear as he grabbed me in a tight hug and ruffled my hair. I let him—what else can you do with a hyperactive younger brother?

"It was about damn time, Luke," he said. "I was waiting for you to pop the question, and you were taking so long I started considering doing it myself..." I rolled my eyes at his words, but I knew it was his way of showing support. I couldn't have asked for a more supportive family, and that was something I was eternally grateful for. It was the kind of support I hoped to provide for our children when Luce and I decided to take that step. I hoped that would be sooner rather than later.

Landon was the last one to congratulate me. I expected him to caution me—to urge me to think things through and not rush, like he usually did—but instead, he shook my hand firmly, and a small smile curved his lips.

"Congratulations, Luke. I'm happy for Luce and you."

I arched my brow, suspicious about the lack of any advice-giving commentary. "No advice?"

Landon chuckled. "No advice. You know what you're doing. You love her, and she loves you. I can only hope to find a love like yours someday." I wanted to assure him that would happen soon, but to be honest, I had never seen or even heard him date a girl or even talk about one.

"Thank you. That means a lot."

Once everyone had offered their congratulations, my mom jumped right back into action, already planning the wedding in her head. "Luke, I want to help out with the wedding as much as possible. I don't want to intrude, but I'd be delighted to assist with anything you need. I have some great catering contacts that might come in handy. I'm guessing Eve will handle the floral arrangements? That's a wise choice—she creates the most beautiful bouquets I've ever seen…"

At some point, I tuned out, overwhelmed by happiness, as a single realization settled in my mind. *I am going to make Luce my wife soon.*

Once I managed to get my mom to stop discussing wedding plans, I headed back home to check on my future wife. While I was at my parents' place, she sent me a few updates, letting me know she was feeling better. Still, I was eager to return and be by her side.

Especially since I had a special delivery for her.

"Hey, Luce," I called out as I entered our home. Right away, I heard scrambling in the living room. Earlier this morning, I had insisted that she wait until I got back to open today's slot. She agreed, but I could tell she was running out of patience. "Missed me?" I asked, leaning down to kiss her. She returned the kiss tenderly but quickly pulled back, a guilty look in her eyes.

"I have a confession to make…"

"Uh-oh…"

She sighed softly, holding up her hands in defense. "I'm bad. I know! I couldn't help myself. You were gone for too long…" Luce held a small note in my handwriting that read, *'I told you to wait for me before opening this,'* accompanied by a poorly drawn winky emoji that looked defective at its best.

The message was there for a good reason. I didn't want Luce to find the scrapbook I had prepared, so I took it to my parents' home. Part of my visit there today was to retrieve it.

"I'm sorry, I couldn't help myself. I know you told me to wait, but I just got too impatient…" She pressed her lips into a thin line, clearly worried about my reaction now that she had opened the sixth slot.

"Sweetheart, relax. It's perfectly fine. Besides, I have your present right here." While I was good at giving presents, I couldn't say the same about wrapping them. My execution was poor at best, but it was what was inside that counted. Her face brightened as she took the messily wrapped present from me and hopped onto the couch.

I enjoyed seeing this more relaxed version of her around me. I worried there would always be a certain degree of guard after I had broken her heart, but she looked like she could completely relax around me now…and that was all I wanted.

Luce wasted no time as she ripped the paper open, finding a dotted, black-and-white scrapbook in her hands. She looked at me, clearly confused, before her gaze darted back toward the notebook again. Her eyebrows furrowed as she tried to piece together what it was.

People always told you to get rid of everything you shared once your relationship ended—but I knew that could never be the case with us. Even if we never got back together, I wanted to have countless memories to hold on to when things got hard. So, I kept everything from our time together ten years ago: multiple photographs we had taken together, movie tickets, date night grocery receipts that had long faded, notes she had written to me over the years, and even wrappers of her favorite candy. My scrapbooking skills weren't the best, either, though I liked to believe I made up for it with the way I could handle wood. Still, I tried to place everything together so it looked aesthetically nice.

Luce flipped over the first page, already nearly in tears, as her eyes found an image of us on our first date. We had asked a stranger to take a picture of us, and we were grinning from ear to ear. I had more planned to remind her of the first date we shared, but I thought that was a nice photo to open up the scrapbook of our memories.

"I have no words…" she whispered, flipping the page as she examined what was inside. I wrapped my arm around her, holding her close.

"Luckily for you, I hear kisses also express feelings well," I teased, leaning in to kiss her cheek softly. She tilted her head to look up at me, and I dipped my head lower to meet her lips. We shared a tender kiss, yet it was enough to make my stomach swirl with butterflies. With her by my side, I knew I would never stop feeling like this, even after another ten years had passed.

Chapter 7
Lucy

"ALL RIGHT," Luke said as I reached for the seventh slot in my calendar. Every day I spent by his side was present enough, but I couldn't deny that these past seven days had been incredible. He gave me something to look forward to every day, and none of the presents he got for me were the low-effort, casual kind. No, it took money, time, and effort to plan them out, and Luke was more than happy to do that to make me smile. "I have to warn you. These next two slots are more action-based, so if you're not feeling well..." He trailed off, concern present in his eyes.

"I'm feeling perfectly fine, don't worry." I shook my head, feeling like the stomach bug was a distant memory. I was eager for more dates with Luke, though I might give pasta a break for a while. I quickly tore off the wrapping paper to reveal another note—this time, a small envelope with Luke's handwriting that read, *'Let's go back to the beginning…'*

Opening the envelope, I found two tickets for the ice rink that Port Cartier set up every year. Luke really meant it when he said we'd revisit our beginnings because this was where our first date took place. I could vividly recall that day—how nervous I was for my first date ever. My mom had a good feeling about it, and she was right. It turned out to be the best date I could have asked for.

"There's no way...They still do this?" I asked, my eyes wide with surprise. The last time I had been ice skating was exactly ten years ago, so I wasn't overly confident in my skills.

"They do," he confirmed with a nod. "And we're going to ice skate tonight."

I didn't know how he made it happen, but Luke had us enter the ice rink after it had officially closed. Ten years ago, we had first skated and then enjoyed a cup of hot cocoa. This time, we reversed the order: we started with hot cocoa and donuts to gain our strength, and once the rink was cleared and shut down, it was our turn.

In all honesty, it hadn't surprised me *that* much. Luke was still well-loved in town, so he probably pulled a few strings to make this special evening possible. He helped me put on rental ice skates before lacing up his own, and then we moved onto the ice. My lack of experience showed immediately; if not for his firm grip on my hand, I would've slipped.

"Luke!" I squealed as I struggled to keep my balance.

"I've got you, sweetheart. Don't worry. Just try to relax," he assured me in his soothing voice, gliding effortlessly across the ice. At that moment, he was more dragging me along than I was putting in any effort.

"How are you so good at this?" I asked, still tense as I let him guide me. Fearing another slip, I did minimal legwork, relying entirely on him to keep us steady.

"I've been coming here for the past ten years. This place has always reminded me of you," Luke explained, and I had to fight the urge to cry again. Seriously, what was up with me? After our breakup, I cried so much it felt like my tears were permanently dried up. For the past decade, I'd kept my emotions in check and rarely cried. Yet now, by his side, I found myself crying happy tears almost every day. Maybe I should consult with Landon; this couldn't be normal.

"I will need you to relax a little and start moving your legs. It's like regular skating, just a little more slippery. I know you can skate, so I know you can do this too." He loosened his grip on my hand, and I drew in a sharp breath, encouraged by his words.

Maybe I could do this...

The moment he released me and I tried to move my left leg, I slipped on the ice and landed squarely on my backside with a loud thud. The pain was faint but enough to make me groan.

Luke approached me carefully, his expression serious, but he was clearly struggling to hold back laughter.

"Stop laughing!" I accused him, trying to stay stern.

"I'm not laughing!" he retorted as he raised his hands in the air, though his voice betrayed him, and he burst into laughter.

Shaking my head, I grabbed him by his pants and tugged him toward me so he landed on the ice, tumbling over me. Now, neither of us could stop laughing, the sound echoing deep into the night.

Last night's ice-skating date left a few bruises on my body, but they were all worth it. I had so much fun that my stomach hurt from how hard I had laughed. The faint muscle pain from laughing also extended to today, but I was ready to do it all over again.

Still snuggled in bed beneath the blankets, I watched as Luke brought over the present for the eighth day of his Advent calendar. I was looking forward to another evening spent with him. While I loved the thoughtful gifts he had been giving me, it was the time we spent together that was the greatest gift of all.

The small box landed in my hands, and Luke gave me a playful wink, encouraging me to open it.

"Go on," he urged with a grin. As I unwrapped the paper, I found another envelope inside. The note read, *'Still at the beginning.'* I eyed him curiously, trying to figure out which memorable date this could be tied to. With so many special moments between us, it was hard to narrow it down.

When I opened the envelope, the realization set in. It was a ticket to Port-Cartier's tiny cinema that only played one movie a week. While I had passed by it a few times, I didn't think they were still in business. Port-Cartier was a small town, but it offered plenty of activities to do.

This was another of our dates when we first started seeing each other. Luke made sure to take me out somewhere at least once a week. Sometimes, it was to the movies or ice-skating; other times, we'd settle at our favorite spots and enjoy the view together. Both were equally special.

"The movies..." was all I managed to say before Luke cut in.

"Check out what movie's playing."

I glanced down once more, my eyes widening in surprise. *"Monkeys Against the World*? Luke! How did you make this happen? They stopped showing this movie over a decade ago..." I shook my head in disbelief. First, the ice rink, and now this? It was like he had some kind of magical power, because there was no way he could pull off these surprises on his own.

"A man in love always has his ways." Luke smirked. "And if you remember the full date…"

I finished his thought. "We also went to the arcade after the movie. You won me a teddy bear I kept at my mom's house."

"Now you know how that date will finish."

A smirk spread across my face as I met his gaze. "I'm not sure you're right about that. I think it might end upstairs, in our bedroom, with you buried deep inside me…"

The *Monkeys Against the World* movie was just as terrible as I remembered, but it held a special place in my heart. It would always be one of my favorite movies, especially when I had Luke's arm wrapped around me throughout the film, both times I watched it. I didn't think I'd ever enjoyed a movie in the theater as much as I did tonight.

Afterward, we headed to the arcade, which was small but offered plenty of games to keep us entertained for a better portion of the night—until it shut down at one in the morning.

"You know, I often thought of this arcade when I was away," I admitted. It was yet another thing I refused to enjoy after our breakup. After not having enjoyed it for so long, it hit me all at once. The lights, the noise, the laughter. It was just as I remembered.

"Me too," Luke stated, linking his hand with mine. "I knew you would be back here with me someday. Now, if you'll excuse me…I have a teddy bear to win for the love of my life."

Chapter 8
Luke

WITH THE PROPOSAL just days away, my nerves had finally kicked in. It wasn't the act of proposing that made me anxious but the pressure of ensuring everything was perfect for Luce. She deserved nothing less, and that was exactly what I intended to give her.

To keep her from suspecting anything, I spent most of the ninth day of my Advent calendar helping her decorate our house. She was fully immersed in the Christmas spirit. We had strung up more Christmas lights than I'd ever imagined, covering almost every inch of our home. I thought we were done once the lights were up *around* the house, but I quickly realized how wrong I was.

"This looks great," she beamed, draping the mistletoe around the fireplace. Since I hadn't decorated for Christmas before, we had to go out and buy everything from scratch, but it was worth every minute. Watching her face light up with the Christmas lights and tiny figurines made me wish we could celebrate Christmas more often than just once a year.

"It does," I agreed, adjusting another strand of lights from the top of my ladder. "But shouldn't we hang it a bit higher? That way, we can kiss beneath it."

She turned to me with a mischievous smile that nearly made me lose my balance.

"Are you saying you're opposed to sex in front of the fireplace?" she teased.

"No, ma'am. In fact, I think it's a fantastic idea…" I replied, though my gaze kept drifting to the clock above the fireplace. Luce had been eager to open the ninth slot of her Advent calendar that morning, but I had to gently hold her off since today's present was time-sensitive.

I'd asked Sailor to arrive at exactly four p.m. It was now 3:59 p.m., so it was finally time for Luce to get her gift. I descended the stairs and gestured toward the remaining slots on the calendar.

"You can open your slot now, sweetheart. I think you've waited long enough," I said, watching with a grin as Luce immediately dropped the mistletoe. *Talk about priorities.* She dashed over to the coffee table and tore open the ninth slot with eager anticipation. Her excitement came to a sudden confused halt when she pulled out a photo of her and Sailor.

She looked at the photograph, then back at me, and then at the photo again, her expression radiating confusion. I savored every moment, knowing what was about to unfold.

"This is a very lovely photo of me and Sailor, thank you…" she started, her voice trailing off as she tried to piece together what was happening. "Though I must admit, it does feel a bit random…" Her gaze continued to dart between me and the photograph she held in her hands, clearly unsure of what was happening.

I rubbed my forehead and shrugged. "Oh, I'm sorry. The real thing just didn't fit into the calendar."

At that moment, the front door burst open, and Sailor's voice rang out with excitement. "Surprise!" She jumped up and down, her blonde hair bouncing with each bounce, and her brown eyes locked onto Luce. She had a massive red bow on her head. "Merry Christmas!"

Luce stood frozen, her shock evident. She looked between Sailor and me, as if she was trying to convince herself this was actually happening. "What...what's happening?" she stammered, overwhelmed by the sudden turn of events.

Sailor dashed toward Luce, practically throwing herself into her arms. Luce managed to catch her, though they both stumbled backward. I reached out to steady Luce with a supportive hand on her back.

"Oh, my God," Luce finally exclaimed, her voice choked with emotion. "What—how did—oh, my God!" Tears welled up in her eyes as she held Sailor tightly, not letting go. "I was just thinking today that this was our first Christmas apart! I missed you so much. I can't believe this!" Her sobs made her words hard to understand, and Sailor, consequently, started crying as well.

"I know!" Sailor sniffled. "I was thinking the same thing. Then your boyfriend contacted me and said he wanted to fly me over." I froze, a wave of panic washing over me. With both of them so emotional, I feared she might accidentally reveal something she wasn't supposed to.

"He wanted you to have the best Christmas ever," Sailor continued, "and he insisted that I should be here to make it happen."

My shoulders relaxed with relief, and I shot Sailor a grateful look, mouthing, 'Thank you.' Neither of them could stop crying, but I was determined to check if everything went well. I was worried that Luce might see us exchange messages or something, so I kept our communication to a minimum.

"Did everything go well with your trip?" I asked.

Sailor nodded, wiping away a tear. "Yeah, everything went great. The flight was smooth, and Landon came to pick me up...though I'm not entirely sure he likes me."

I gave her a reassuring smile. "That's just how Landon is.

Don't overthink it. Most of the time, we're not sure if he likes anything or anyone besides his job…"

Sailor took a small breath before continuing, "Anyway, I'm staying with Eve, which is amazing. And Ed is great, too. I can see why Eve adores him so much. But what about you?" Her eyes turned to Luce, filled with genuine curiosity. "How have you been? Tell me everything…"

I watched them for a moment longer, and then I knew it was time for me to retreat and give them some time to catch up. I was finally at peace now that I made Sailor's visit happen, and the sheer joy on Luce's face made it all worth it.

Sailor didn't leave until late into the night, but I didn't mind. Luce and she spent the whole day catching up, while I took on the role of unofficial caterer, ordering takeout and regularly bringing drinks to keep them going. It was fascinating to watch them—the way they were wrapped up in their own little world, barely noticing my presence. It wasn't until Sailor left for Eve's place and Luce showered and got ready for bed that the bubble finally burst.

She hopped into bed, the mattress bouncing beneath her, and I set aside the book I had been holding, ready to focus on her. The smile on her face was still as present as it had been hours earlier when Sailor arrived at our home.

"Did you have fun today, sweetheart?" I asked, my voice gentle. The way she snuggled into me, holding me close, was answer enough, but I was eager to hear all about her impressions.

"I had *so* much fun. I can't believe you made all of this happen. It means so much to me that I get to have my best friend here for my first Christmas away from Seattle. Thank you, thank you, thank you," she said, her words punctuated by a flood of grateful kisses. I wrapped my arm around her, tracing gentle circles on her back.

"I'm glad you had fun," I replied with a smile. "But I'm feeling particularly generous tonight. If you want to, you can open your slot for tomorrow morning."

Her eyes widened with excitement, and her face lit up as if she couldn't quite believe the words she'd just heard. "Are you serious?"

I didn't respond; instead, I handed over the slot for the tenth day. She wasted no time questioning whether she should save the moment for tomorrow. Before I could say another word, the paper was ripped off, and she revealed another notebook, this time with a floral pattern. As she opened it, the first page read a few simple words—*100 reasons why I love you.*

Her lips parted, and she flipped another page open, listing endless reasons why I loved her so much. The reasons ranged from the obvious—her soul, her beauty, her sense of humor— to the more personal touches, like the way she made sure my pancakes were always slightly burned because she knew that's how I liked them or the playful arguments we had over my choice of shower gel.

A small swallow disrupted her throat before she looked up at me, capturing my chin between her fingers, and leaning up to kiss me. That kiss was all it took for us to unlock the desire that needed to be satisfied. In a heartbeat, she placed the notebook on her bedside table, and then she was on top of me. I didn't need her to hear her say *'thank you.'*

The way she kissed me said enough.

It was urgent. Hungry. Like she couldn't handle another second away from me.

I grasped the hem of her shirt, pulling it over her head so most of her body was revealed to me, with the exception of the thin panties that she wore. Her hands pulled my boxers down, and my cock sprung free right away, ready to be buried deep inside her.

"Come here, sweetheart," I murmured against her lips as I tugged her panties to the side—not even having the time to remove them properly—and then I slid myself inside her in one long stroke.

She clenched around me, massaging my cock from all angles, as a small moan escaped her lips, bleeding into the kiss we shared.

"Fuck," I grunted, my broad arms grasping her slender body and pulling her in closer. I wanted every inch of her body pressed up against mine as she rode me. I wanted to taste her kiss on my lips, to lose myself in her intoxicating scent, to feel the presence of her skin against mine.

Luce moved her hips in a controlled, circular motion that drove us both insane. "Just like that, Luce. My God...." I tensed against her, feeling every cell in my body awaken with desire. It was just the effect she had on me.

The small whimpers that left her lips as she soaked me in her arousal were driving me insane, getting my cock impossibly harder. One of my hands grasped her ass, while the other reached in between her thighs, rubbing her clit slowly.

"Oh, Luke...oh, God," she panted. Our lips separated, only for her to bury her face in my neck to stifle her moans—though I could hear them that much more clearly with her lips right below my ear.

"That's right. Ride my cock, just like that," I continued to praise her as if that was the only thing my mind could have thought to say. I was that *lost* in her. Her thighs were trembling around me, pussy clenching around my cock as it hit that spot inside her that she enjoyed. We were both caught in a frenzy neither of us could snap ourselves out of.

"More...please, *more*," she pleaded, and I took that as a cue to flip us over. My cock remained buried deep inside her as I moved on top of her, now able to thrust harder. Faster.

One of my hands continued to apply pressure to her clit, while the other held her thigh open as I moved deeply inside her, causing her to shake uncontrollably.

"Luke!" Her hands grasped my back, as if that would've helped her to anchor herself through the sensation we were both trapped in. I leaned down, trailing tender kisses over her chest, all the way up to throat and her chin.

"Good God, you feel so good," was all I managed to say before I could feel her tighten in the way she usually did before she came. She let out one last moan, arching herself beneath me, before her pleasure struck her, causing shudders to roll through her entire body. Luce could barely catch a breath, with the sheer pleasure radiating from her face, and that triggered my orgasm. I slammed myself inside her two more times before I shot my load into her, buckling on top of her from the sudden sensation that had overcome me. I let out a loud grunt, gasping for air like she did, and needing a moment to recover. Still, I could not refrain from giving her another kiss. She was my entire world, right in my hands.

Chapter 9

Lucy

"I DON'T THINK Landon is overly fond of me," Sailor told me the next morning when we met to catch up again. I couldn't get enough of her presence. Now that she was next to me again, I could feel physically how much I had missed her. A part of me wished she could stay here, in Port-Cartier, forever, but the rest of me knew this time would come to an end, so I wanted to make the most of it.

"Oh, come on. It couldn't have been that bad..." I rubbed her shoulder, trying to comfort her. It was hard to imagine anyone not liking my best friend. She was a ray of sunshine wherever she went, and she could draw people in so easily. I highly doubted that Landon was immune to her charm. Maybe she misread the situation.

"It was *that* bad," she continued as we strolled by the shore. Despite the winter chill that had wrapped around the town, I wanted her to see everything it offered. Thankfully, this time, she was staying a few days. The waves lulled softly around the sandy beach, reflecting the soft shades of orange and purple. "I'm telling you. I got off the plane and saw this cute guy holding a sign with my name. And I was thinking —*well, this is a great start to this trip.* I introduced myself and started asking questions. I did everything you're meant to do when you arrive somewhere new, but he kept all communication to a minimum. I couldn't help but feel like I was annoying him…"

It was hard to believe that their first encounter went like that, but then again, Landon was the most introverted of all the brothers. So maybe there was some truth to what she was saying—I couldn't tell.

"And I'm going to keep seeing him, because—" She paused and then shook her head. "I intend to visit you more, and he is your boyfriend's brother. I seriously miss you more than any words can describe, girl. Seattle isn't the same without you there."

Her words struck me right at my heart. My eyes welled up, and I could barely contain the tears that formed there. Suddenly, I was overcome by this massive sadness that I couldn't control, knowing that things would never be the same. Luke was the best thing to ever happen to me, but Sailor was the close second. She had been there when I had no one—my best friend, biggest cheerleader, and platonic soulmate.

"Oh, don't cry! You're going to make me cry!" she mumbled, pulling me into a tight hug. I didn't release her for a good minute, and I likely wouldn't have if it weren't for the sickness that continued to rise in my stomach.

"God. I feel sick again…" I murmured, shaking my head. "Speaking of the devil, I actually think I'm going to have to see Landon to get some blood work done, because this doesn't seem normal anymore. I've been sick for days. It comes and goes, and nothing seems to help…" I pulled back, only to face Sailor, who was staring at me with wide eyes.

"What?"

"Okay, don't kill me, but…have you considered that pregnancy may be an option here?"

My heart dropped to my stomach. *No, I hadn't considered*

that as an option. And I don't even know why. Luke and I had talked about kids, and we both agreed that we wanted to have two someday in the future, but I always assumed it would be down the line when we were more settled in. But, to be fair, we didn't use condoms, and only relied on tracking my ovulation as a method of protection.

If it isn't the consequences of your actions, a voice in my head rang as I remained speechless.

"Judging by your face, I'm guessing that's possible…" Sailor drew in a sharp breath. "All right, we're not going to panic prematurely. We're going to get you a pregnancy test, and you are going to take the moment you get home. I'll be there with you, don't worry."

I hooked my arm around hers, drawing her closer, as if to wrap us with some secrecy. "I can't just go in and buy a pregnancy test. Everyone knows everyone here, and people are going to talk. Luke may find out I'm pregnant—*if I am*—before I even have the chance to tell him. That's the extent of how quickly the gossip spreads around here."

Sailor nodded, staring at me with the look of a woman on a mission. "I got you. I will take one for the team. I'll go to the store, and I'll buy a pack of pregnancy tests, so you're set for life."

I waited for Sailor in the car while she purchased the pregnancy tests at our local store. It took her a good ten minutes before she emerged from the store, triumphantly holding up the bag that concealed the pregnancy tests inside. Her smile stretched from ear to ear, but I was on edge, barely able to think without feeling like I might throw up.

The weight of the moment was overwhelming. I knew if

the test turned out positive, it would all work out. I had no doubt that Luke would be an incredible father, but the reality of it all hit me hard. We had only recently moved in together and had been back for just a few months. The idea of this happening so soon was unexpected, and I wasn't sure how to process it all.

"I've secured the goods," my best friend told me as she hopped in the car. "No one will be able to track these pregnancy tests to you, so your secret is safe. There's no need to worry."

I smiled softly, feeling a flicker of relief. Starting the car, I was eager to get home and finally take the test. I was thankful Luke was at work because one look would be enough for him to know something was wrong. And I didn't want him to worry in case this was nothing—in case I wasn't pregnant.

"Sailor...what am I going to do if I'm pregnant? I've only just moved to Port-Cartier..." I said, my voice laced with worry. I kept my eyes focused on the road as I drove, feeling a knot tighten in my stomach.

"What do you mean, what are you going to do? Luce, you're going to be the best mom ever. And Luke will be a great dad, too. You two are a match made in heaven. That baby is going to have the best parents ever. Yes, maybe it's happening a little sooner than you expected, but I believe in divine timing. What's meant to happen, will happen, and you've just got to roll with it," Sailor said, her words spilling out rapidly as if she wanted to chase away any lingering doubts. "Besides, you have his family and yours here. You have a whole support system ready for you. You won't be alone in this."

I glanced over at Sailor, feeling the tears prick at the corners of my eyes. "Yeah, but I don't have my best friend here. That's what I'm missing."

Sailor smiled as she reached out to rub my arm. "We'll figure it out," she said gently. "We can organize things better and find a way to see each other more often. I miss you so much, too; sometimes, it feels like I might go crazy from it."

Before we could continue with our conversation, we pulled up in front of the house. Both of us rushed inside as if our lives depended on it. I could hardly breathe by the time I reached the bathroom, fumbling with the packaging. Sailor stood beside me, watching me.

"Do you think you can pee on your own, or should I stay for moral support?" she asked seriously.

"I think I'll manage to pee on my own, but we'll wait for the results together, okay?"

She exited the bathroom, giving me some much-needed privacy as she gently shut the door behind her. I took a deep breath, grateful for the plastic cups she'd brought along—they made handling the test a little less daunting.

I was so nervous that it took a minute before I was ready to see Sailor again. I opened the door, my knees weak, and stared at my best friend. It was hard to believe that one simple test would determine the course of the rest of my life.

She grabbed my hands, holding them tightly, as if she wanted to draw off some of the anxiety that I felt. It wasn't just anxiety, I realized. It was also…excitement. Maybe having a baby right now wouldn't be such a bad idea. It would undoubtedly be a major change, but there was no one I felt safer with than Luke. We could handle this together. The thought of him holding a tiny baby we created together filled my chest with so much warmth that I couldn't think about anything else.

"Just so you know," Sailor started, breaking the silence, "if you're pregnant, I'm totally claiming godmother rights."

A burst of laughter escaped me, so loud it quickly turned into a snort, and soon, neither of us could stop laughing. It was one of those moments of pure joy where words seemed to escape me entirely. Sailor was here, and I was with Luke again. What more could I ask for?

The five minutes we had to wait flew by, and we retreated back to the bathroom to check the white test. By then, my hands were shaking so much that I had to turn to Sailor for support.

"You check it first," I urged her. "I don't think I can."

Sailor didn't need any more encouragement. She stepped forward, lifted the test from the cup, and glanced at me before her eyes fell on the result. Sailor's poker face was nonexistent, and her reaction showed right then. Her eyes widened, her mouth dropped open, and she started bouncing up and down with unrestrained joy.

"You're pregnant!" she screeched, leaping towards me. Overwhelmed by the news and a whirlwind of emotions, I couldn't help but jump with her. My mind was spinning, and I was barely able to keep up. For a moment, a wave of nausea threatened to pull me under, but my emotions swept it away. Tears filled our eyes as Sailor wrapped me in a tight embrace, holding on as if to anchor us both in this moment.

I wasn't sure how long we had been bouncing around like two giddy schoolgirls, but once our laughter subsided, I knew exactly how I wanted to break the news to Luke. Turning to Sailor with a small, excited smile, I shared my plan. "I think I'm going to tell him at the Christmas Eve dinner, with everyone gathered around."

Chapter 10
Luke

TOMORROW WAS THE DAY. It was hard to believe how quickly time had passed. After ten years apart, we were finally about to get engaged. I couldn't wait to see that ring on her finger, symbolizing the rest of our lives together. There was truly no man luckier than me.

"Excuse me, sir," Luce called from behind me. I had been so lost in my morning daydream while making coffee that I hadn't noticed her sneak up on me. Ever since Sailor arrived in Port-Cartier, she had been spending less time at home and more with her. I was happy for her, though her absence felt a bit strange, especially considering how much time we had spent together over the past few months.

"Mm?" I turned around, wrapping my arms around her. I leaned down, kissing her lips multiple times to make up for some of the lost time. Instantly, a smile spread across her face, infectious enough to make me smile back. "How may I be of assistance today?" I asked.

"You're forgetting about my Advent calendar..." she grumbled, her brows furrowing adorably as a slight pout formed on her lips.

"Is that so? It's only morning, sweetheart. The day's only getting started."

Luce shook her head. "Not for me. I've been up since five."

I tilted my head to the side. Usually, she liked to sleep until at least eight, so this was odd. "That's early. Why have you been up so early?

She stepped back with a small sigh. "I couldn't sleep. I've...been having trouble sleeping lately." Her shoulders slumped as she spoke. I linked my hand with hers and guided her toward the remains of the Advent calendar. The eleventh slot was already placed underneath the Christmas tree we had decorated before Sailor arrived. I had seen her inspecting its shape and size, trying to figure out what it was, but she wasn't allowed to touch it. At last, I gestured toward the long item clumsily wrapped in the same wrapping paper. While I wasn't the most skilled at wrapping presents, I at least tried to stick to the Christmas theme.

"What is this?" she asked, retrieving her present. It didn't take her long to unwrap it, her eyes widening with curiosity as she found a massive piece of paper rolled up.

"You'll have to open it to find out..." I said, watching her intrigue grow. As she unrolled it, she found a detailed map of our town. It had taken me a while to mark all the memorable spots, but I made sure to include everything linked to our relationship that I could remember. There was the ice rink where our first date took place, the cinema and the arcade, our spot in the forest, our high school, her mom's flower shop, the path we walked down every day after school, our favorite milkshake place that had since closed down, and many others.

Luce stared at the map, her eyes wide with disbelief as she took in all the little spots I had marked. I had also included a few of the more recent places we had visited, wanting to capture memories from after our reconnection, too.

"I thought we could frame it and put it in our living room. I know you're in charge of the décor, and I understand if it doesn't match the aesthetic—"

"Luke," she interrupted me, "don't be silly. This is beautiful. Of course I want it in our living room. I want to see it every day I wake up by your side." She blinked frantically, trying to hold back tears. I kissed each of her cheeks before settling on her nose and placing a kiss there, too.

"I had another idea, too," I continued, elaborating on the intention behind the gift. "I was thinking we could take the map down once a year and add in new spots we visit." Since this was the last gift before I proposed to her, I wanted to make sure it was meaningful, showing that I paid attention and remembered everywhere we had been, even after all those years. My life had changed since she reentered it, in the best way possible, and I wanted to memorize every detail of it.

Luce sniffled, looking like she was about to burst into tears again. Wanting to comfort her, I pulled her into a tight hug, holding her close. She surrendered to the embrace, practically melting into my touch.

It took everything in me not to propose to her on the spot. But I had waited so long; surely I could wait one more day.

"You have been the best thing to ever happen to me, Luce. I want to spend the rest of my life appreciating you for everything you were, everything you are, and everything you will become. I couldn't be any luckier if I tried." The words spilled from my lips without me even meaning to say them. I meant every single word. And tomorrow, I would finally prove it officially.

Chapter 11
Lucy

"LUKE, STOP EATING THE MINI QUICHES!" I scolded him as I caught him—yet again—munching on the appetizers I had spent hours preparing and arranging for the dinner table.

He looked at me with that cheeky grin, the one that showed he was up to no good. He looked so handsome today that I was willing to forgive him for all his culinary crimes—if only he would start behaving from now on.

The Christmas music played softly in the background as I put the final touches on our Christmas Eve dinner. This was my first time hosting a holiday dinner—usually, it would just be me, Sailor, and my mom in my Seattle apartment with a bunch of takeout, since none of us could muster the energy to cook. But I wanted to make a change with this new beginning in Port-Cartier.

I had prepared a lot of food. There were mini quiches—already raided by Luke's wandering hands—stuffed mushrooms, and freshly baked rolls. The main course featured roast ham with fresh herbs, creamy mashed potatoes, honey-glazed carrots, and cranberry sauce. For dessert, I had classic Christmas pudding and a selection of cookies my mom and

Sailor helped me make. All in all, I was happy with how everything turned out despite regularly being sidetracked by Luke's devouring mouth and mischievous hands.

The doorbell rang, signaling that our first guests had arrived.

"I'll get it!" Luke called out, heading towards the door. As he opened it, I could immediately hear my mom and Sailor exclaiming over the delicious smells roaming through our home. I quickly looked around to take everything in. The dinner had been all set on the wooden table Luke had made himself, surrounded by a mix of chairs—we didn't have enough, so we'd borrowed a few from his family. In the corner, our Christmas tree was fully decorated with colorful ornaments and twinkling lights that warmed my heart.

Technically, it was our baby's first Christmas with us, and Luke didn't even know about it yet. I couldn't help but smile at the secret I was keeping, eagerly anticipating the moment I could finally share the big news with everyone but Sailor. The past two days had been difficult—mostly because I had never been good at keeping secrets or surprises from others.

I was worried the entire time that Luke might somehow read my mind and discover he was about to become a father before the perfect moment to share the news arrived. It turned out he had many powers and talents, but mind reading wasn't one of them…yet.

"Oh, pumpkin! This looks beautiful," my mom beamed as she stepped into the dining room. She greeted me with a big hug, handing me a wrapped present. I returned the embrace, holding her close for a moment, while Luke took the present and carefully placed it beneath the tree.

In the back of my mind, I was still aware that there was one day left on my Advent calendar, and I was dying to know what it was. The gifts had been so thoughtful and creative that I was curious to see what he had planned for the grand finale. Still, I pushed that thought aside, focusing instead on the dinner ahead of us.

"Thanks, Mom. Of course, it can't compare to the dinners you organized when I was little, but I tried..." I shrugged with a smile. Mom was known fo her holiday dinner parties. She always went above and beyond. Thankfully she now had Ed to help her out.

Sailor was the next to hug me, her knowing smile hinting at the secret we shared. She was the only person who knew about my pregnancy, and that was such a relief; otherwise, I'd probably have gone insane trying to keep it under wraps from everyone.

"It's even more beautiful," she continued, moving around and taking in everything we had done with the place. Ed joined the hugging train as well. He and my mom had moved in two months ago, and I couldn't be happier for them. Having lived my life without a father and never seeing my mom with anyone else, it filled me with so much joy to see someone fill that void. I couldn't have asked for a better person for that position than Ed.

"She's been excited all day. Maybe we should make this a tradition, huh?" he said as he released me. I smiled warmly, touched by his words.

"That's the plan..." I nudged him.

The doorbell rang again, alerting us of the arrival of Luke's family. Four more people entered our home, and though it was unusual to have so many guests in our dining room at once, it felt exactly like we had envisioned all those years ago when we first joked about this being our first home. We wanted a place where our family could gather and share our most exciting moments, and I couldn't think of anything more memorable than announcing that we would become parents.

"Hey, you two!" Logan grinned as he approached us, bypassing Luke to pull me into a hug. "Ah, it's been a while since we last saw each other! We should make sure that never happens again."

I laughed. "Logan, it's literally been two weeks."

"Two weeks too long." He nudged me playfully. Luke rolled his eyes, but a smile tugged at his lips. His parents joined the gathering, greeting me by hugging me before mingling with my mom and Ed. This was one of the beautiful things about a small town like Port-Cartier. For the most part, everyone knew—and loved—everyone. It made moments like this feel that much more intimate.

Of course, every family had its black sheep, and for ours, it was Landon. He stayed on the periphery after the initial greetings, but I couldn't help noticing how his gaze kept drifting toward Sailor. It was odd—in an unexpected way— and I wasn't quite sure what to make of it. Maybe a glass of wine would help him loosen up those tense doctor's nerves of his.

That was Luke's job—to ensure everyone had a glass of wine in their hand. I had every intention of announcing my pregnancy soon, since there was no way I would be having a single sip of alcohol. As everyone chatted and smiled from ear to ear, the room filled with holiday spirit. My knees felt weak at the thought of what I had to do, but the moment had arrived, and there was no turning back now.

I cleared my throat, looking around the room. From the other side of the table, Sailor looked at me, seeming to say, 'You go, girl.'

"If you'll give me a moment of your time," I began, "as your host, I'd like to share a few words before we start the dinner. First of all, thank you all for coming." All eyes were on me now. Though they belonged to people who loved Luke and me, it felt like the walls were closing in...until I felt Luke's hand on the small of my back. That simple gesture was instantly soothing, easing my nerves just enough to continue. "It means the world to us. After so many years spent apart, it's wonderful to have our family all in one place. We want to make this a tradition, so consider yourselves already invited for next year." A few small laughs and snuffles of amusement came from different corners of the room. "Anyway, a lot has happened this year, and we're thankful for all of it. But there's one more Christmas present I want to share with all of you..." I turned toward Luke, knowing these words were particularly for him. "We're going to be parents."

Instantly, gasps rippled through the room. Somewhere in the back of my mind, I could already hear my mom starting to cry in that dramatic way she was known for. Ed and Sailor were quick to soothe her. On the other side of the room, Linda said, "I knew it! I told you we'd get grandchildren soon!"

But all my attention was on Luke, who stood before me, dumbfounded and speechless. It took him a few seconds to recover before he finally regained some control over his voice.

"We're—do you really mean that?"

I nodded, feeling a flicker of nervousness as I wondered if I had misjudged his reaction. But in just a moment, all my doubts vanished. The widest smile spread across his face, and he scooped me up into his arms, spinning me around with sheer joy.

"We're going to be parents!" he exclaimed. "I'm going to be a dad!"

I let out a relieved laugh, clinging to him tightly as he spun me. "Babe, you're going to need to put me down. I'm still feeling a bit nauseous."

"Right, right. Sorry," Luke quickly apologized, setting me back on my feet before cupping my cheeks in his hands and kissing me passionately. It wasn't like us to show such public displays of affection in front of our parents, but neither of us could contain our joy. His eyes were brimming with tears— the happy kind—and I couldn't even remember the last time I'd seen him cry.

He then turned to Landon. "I'm going to need to have a

Mia Elliot

long talk with you to learn everything there is to know about babies."

Landon tilted his head to the side, his smile still in place. "I don't specialize in pediatrics, Luke."

"Doesn't matter," Luke retorted with a grin. "I'm still going to need your help." He glanced back at me, kissing the top of my head as he held me close. There was a silent agreement between us that we'd discuss this in greater detail soon, but for now, we were simply excited to enjoy the news with everyone.

Luke wiped away his tears and took a moment to compose himself before drawing everyone's attention again, holding up his glass of wine. Sailor had already taken my wine and claimed it for herself, replacing it with cranberry juice that I could enjoy, and I smiled with gratitude. Turning toward Luke, I saw him clear his throat, ready to continue.

"Well, that was unexpected news," Luke began, his voice filled with emotion. "I'm so glad all of you are here to witness it. I can't imagine any news being more exciting than this. I've always dreamed of starting a family with Luce, and this is the perfect beginning. But I'm about to make it even better—or at least, I'll try…"

He turned toward me, and I was momentarily confused. The realization hit me like a bolt of lightning, followed by a rush of panic because I hadn't anticipated this. The look in his eyes said everything I needed to know.

"Luce, you have been the love of my life since the moment I met you all those years ago. Ten years apart couldn't keep us away from each other, and I don't want to spend another second not connected to you in every possible way. I know you are my one true love—you always have been. When I was a teenager, I thought people were exaggerating about their love stories, but I knew it was all real the moment I met you. A love like this can't be compared to anything else in the world. And now, with our child on the way, I'm more certain than ever that this is the perfect time to take this step."

Everything around me seemed to blur as he moved in what felt like slow motion. He placed his glass of wine down and then lowered himself onto one knee. I was in such a state of blissful shock that my knees nearly gave way, but somehow, I managed to stay upright. He pulled out a small velvet box from his pocket, opening it to reveal a silver ring with an oval-cut diamond.

"Luce Milburne, will you marry me?"

The answer came in an instant, without a moment's hesitation. I didn't even need to think about it; before I could fully process my response, the words were out of my mouth. "Yes! Yes, of course, I'll marry you!" I choked out, watching as he carefully slid the ring onto my finger—a task made all the more difficult with how much my hands were shaking.

The room erupted into applause, and I couldn't shake the feeling that everyone knew about this beforehand. Not a single person in the room—except for me—seemed genuinely surprised by his proposal. They were in awe, certainly, but surprise? Absolutely not.

Luke stood up, wrapping me in his arms and kissing me once more. I was overwhelmed with so much emotion that drawing in a steady breath felt almost impossible.

"I can't wait to spend the rest of my life by your side," he whispered against my lips. "This is my final present of your Advent calendar this year."

With teary eyes, I smiled through my joy. I never thought happy endings were possible, yet on this Christmas Eve, I got proof that mine was undeniably happening.

acknowledgments

First, I just want to say thank you for reading this book! This story originally started as the epilogue to *Broken Promises*, but it kept growing and growing. To do this story justice I knew I had to put it into its own book. I hope you loved Luke and Lucy's story. Don't worry they'll make an appearance or two in the other Port-Cartier books!

If you haven't done so already, please consider leaving a review. It helps more than you know.

I had so much support writing this book. It wouldn't have been possible without the help from the people below.

To my family - Thank you for being supportive of my dream and celebrating every time something happens with my books whether its big or small.

To AB - Thank you for lifting me up, listening to all my ramblings, and encouraging me every step of the way.

To DerpyWickedFox Editorial, thank you for polishing this book and making it shine.

To Florence and the whole team at Happily Booked PR, I couldn't have done this without you. Thank you for helping me to promote my books.

To Aida at Algart, thank you for making the most beautiful cover and perfectly capturing Lucy and Luke during Christmas.

To Sara at Sara's Design Services, thank you for formatting this book. Your designs perfectly capture the book's essence.

also by mia elliot

about the author

Growing up in a small town in Maine, Mia's childhood was full of countless books filled with love stories, adventure, mystery, and, at times, magic. Her love for these tales grew into a passion for story-telling and filling uncounted notebook pages with vibrant characters.

Through the busyness and stresses of life, Mia always returns to her characters and imagined places, keeping writing as her passion and her outlet to unwind, recharge, and recenter.